For my mother, who had to wear a yellow dress, long ago —E.J.

For Natalia —T.B.

Text copyright © 2007 by Emily Jenkins
Pictures copyright © 2007 by Tomek Bogacki
All rights reserved
Distributed in Canada by Douglas & McIntyre Ltd.
Color separations by Embassy Graphics
Printed and bound in the United States of America
by Phoenix Color Corporation
Designed by Barbara Grzeslo
First edition, 2007
10 9 8 7 6 5 4 3 2 1

www.fsgkidsbooks.com

Library of Congress Cataloging-in-Publication Data
Jenkins, Emily.
    Daffodil, crocodile / Emily Jenkins ; pictures by Tomek Bogacki.— 1st ed.
        p.   cm.
    Summary: Tired of being one of three look-alike sisters that no one can tell
apart, Daffodil puts on a papier-mâché crocodile head and has her own individual
adventures.
    ISBN-13: 978-0-374-39944-3
    ISBN-10: 0-374-39944-1
    [1. Individuality—Fiction. 2. Sisters—Fiction. 3. Imagination—Fiction.
4. Triplets—Fiction.] I. Bogacki, Tomasz, ill. II. Title.

PZ7.J5 Dafc 2007
[E]—dc22

2005040163

Daffodil, CROCODILE

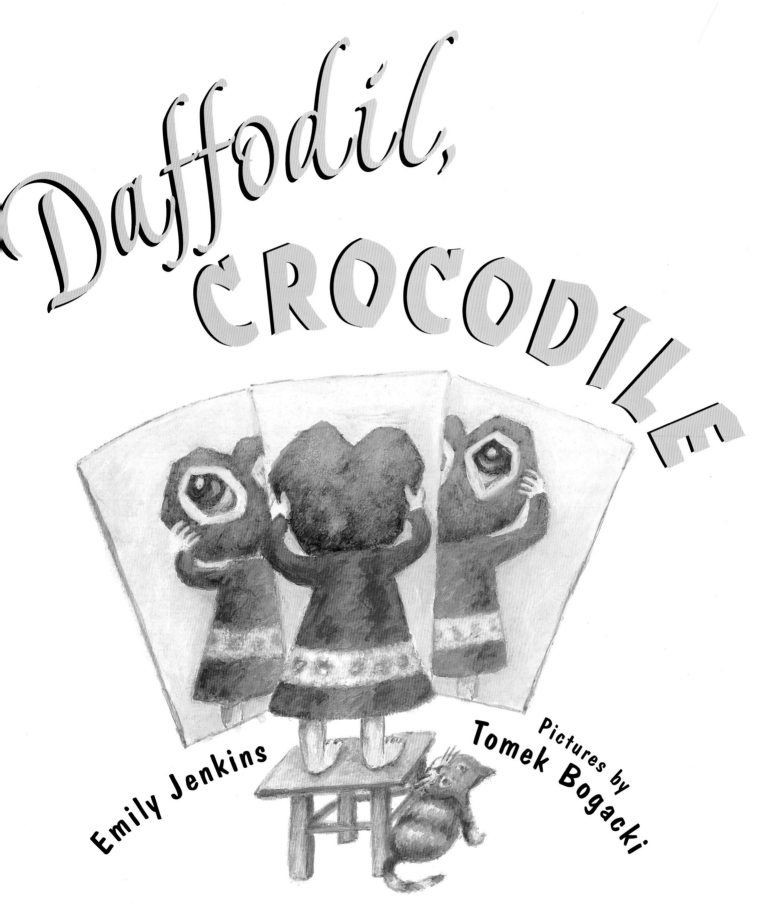

Emily Jenkins

Pictures by
Tomek Bogacki

Frances Foster Books
Farrar, Straus and Giroux
New York

Daffodil had two sisters,
and they all three
looked alike.
No one could tell
them apart.
Not even Mommy
sometimes.
But Daffodil
always could.
And Violet and
Rose could, too.

"They're such NICE little girls,"
said Mommy's friends.
"So clean.
So pretty.
So quiet.
Like a bouquet of flowers."

"**What about me?**"
said Daffodil.
"That's you," they said.
"A pretty little,
clean little
flower of a girl."

At school, when Daffodil
raised her hand in circle time,
the teacher said,
"Rose, what do you have
to share?"

"It's not me," said Rose.

"I'm sorry. VIOLET,
what do you have to share?"

"It's not me," said Violet.

"I'm sorry," the teacher said.
"DAFFODIL, you have
your hand up. What do you
have to share?"

"Never mind," said
Daffodil. "I forgot."

One day, Cynthia and Daffodil
built a block city.
"Rose," said Cynthia,
"let's get the cars out
and make a traffic jam."

"I'm not Rose,"
said Daffodil.

"I know," said Cynthia.

The teacher rang the bell
for lunch.
"I'm sitting with Violet!"
Cynthia cried, grabbing
Daffodil's hand.

"I'm not Violet,"
said Daffodil.

Daffodil's mommy was taking an art class.
She made a drawing, a painting, and a sculpture.
Then she built a crocodile head out of papier-mâché.
"The teeth are so big," said Rose.
"The eyes look mean," said Violet.

Daffodil took the crocodile head and put it on.
"I like it!" she yelled.
"Why?" asked Violet.
"Why?" asked Rose.
"Crocodiles are not flowers,"
said Daffodil.

Raaa
raaa
raaa

Chomp
chomp
chomp

Daffodil wore the crocodile head
all afternoon. The crocodile had adventures.
It took a trip to Jupiter.

It swam across an ocean and
made friends with a blue whale.
It won the world championship at soccer.

Violet and Rose had a tea party,
and the crocodile ate the guests.

At dinner, Mommy said
the crocodile had to say
goodbye.
But the crocodile wouldn't
leave. It ate spaghetti,
spilled its milk,
and stuck
two green beans
up its nose.
"Where's my pretty little,
clean little flower?"
Mommy asked.

The next day, the crocodile
went to school.
"Who's this crocodile?"
asked the teacher.

"It's not me," said Violet.

"It's not me,"
said Rose.

"I'm going to eat everyone
in the block city,"
said the crocodile.

In the playground, the crocodile got very dirty.
It played soccer and scraped its knee.
It climbed to the top of the hill and
was queen of all it could see.

"Daffodil, will you take that head off, please?"
asked the teacher. The crocodile didn't answer.
It was digging a hole with a stick.

"Daffodil, do you want to skip rope?" asked Cynthia. The crocodile didn't answer. It was biting a tree.

"Daffodil, you're being weird," said Violet and Rose. The crocodile just went

Raaa raaa raaa

Chomp chomp chomp

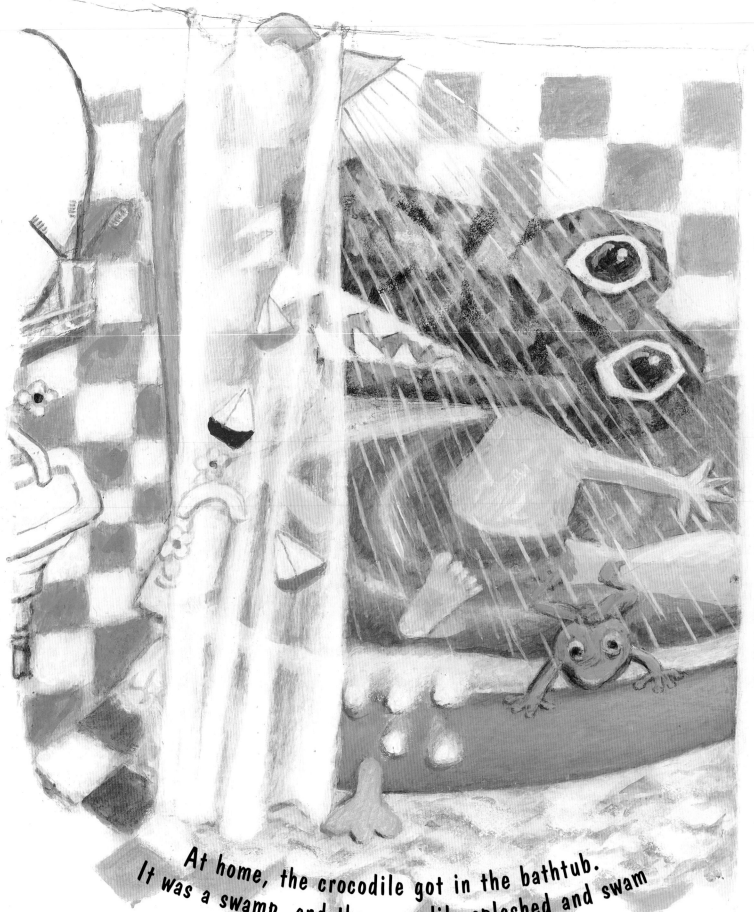

At home, the crocodile got in the bathtub.
It was a swamp, and the crocodile splashed and swam
and got water all over the floor.

When it got out, its head was
falling apart. Its teeth were loose
and its nose was all soggy.
"You have to take the head off,"
said Mommy.
"It's getting ruined."

Daffodil took it off.
"I'm not a flower," she said.
"I'm still a crocodile."
"Oh?" said Mommy.
"A crocodile," said Daffodil.
"Even if I don't have the head."
"Oh," said Mommy.
"I didn't know."

Then she ran off
to swim across the ocean
and play with the other
creatures of the sea.

HKENP   +
         E
JENKI

JENKINS, EMILY
    DAFFODIL, CROCODILE

KENDALL
12/09   DISCARD